THE DOG WHO WISHED HE COULD FLY

DENISE MERIDITH

The Dog Who Wished He Could Fly

Printed in the United States of America

My thanks to Julian Regawa for the illustrations and Bella Media Management for editing.

First Printing, 2019

ISBN Print Paperback: 9781087036502

THE DOG WHO WISHED HE COULD FLY

THE ADVENTURES OF ARRY: VOLUME 1

From the time he was a puppy, Arry wished he was a bird.

Arry would jump and jump and jump. But he never could fly.

Arry often tried to climb up the honeysuckle vine to follow the birds. But he never made it to the top of the wall.

Arry would watch the baby birds playing in the yard. But when he came to play, they would fly away.

One day a grackle asked:
“Why are you so sad?”

“You get to see far-away places,” said Arry. “My Mom and I only walk around the block every day.”

"But we have to fly around all day to only find crumbs," said the Grackle. "Your Mom serves you delicious meals three times a day."

"They all hide from me when I want to play," said Arry.

"We have to protect our babies from harm and the weather," said the Grackle. "You have a nice, soft bed every night."

"The Mockingbirds make fun of me every day," sighed Arry.

"The Mockingbirds have no friends. They are mean and lonely and envious of you. Pay no attention to them, Arry," said the Grackle.

"You all seem to be happy, singing all the time," said Arry.

"We sometimes sing to look for love or because we miss our Moms. Your Mom loves you every hour of every day," said the Grackle.

Arry thought about all the Grackle said that day and realized he is very lucky to be a loved dog.